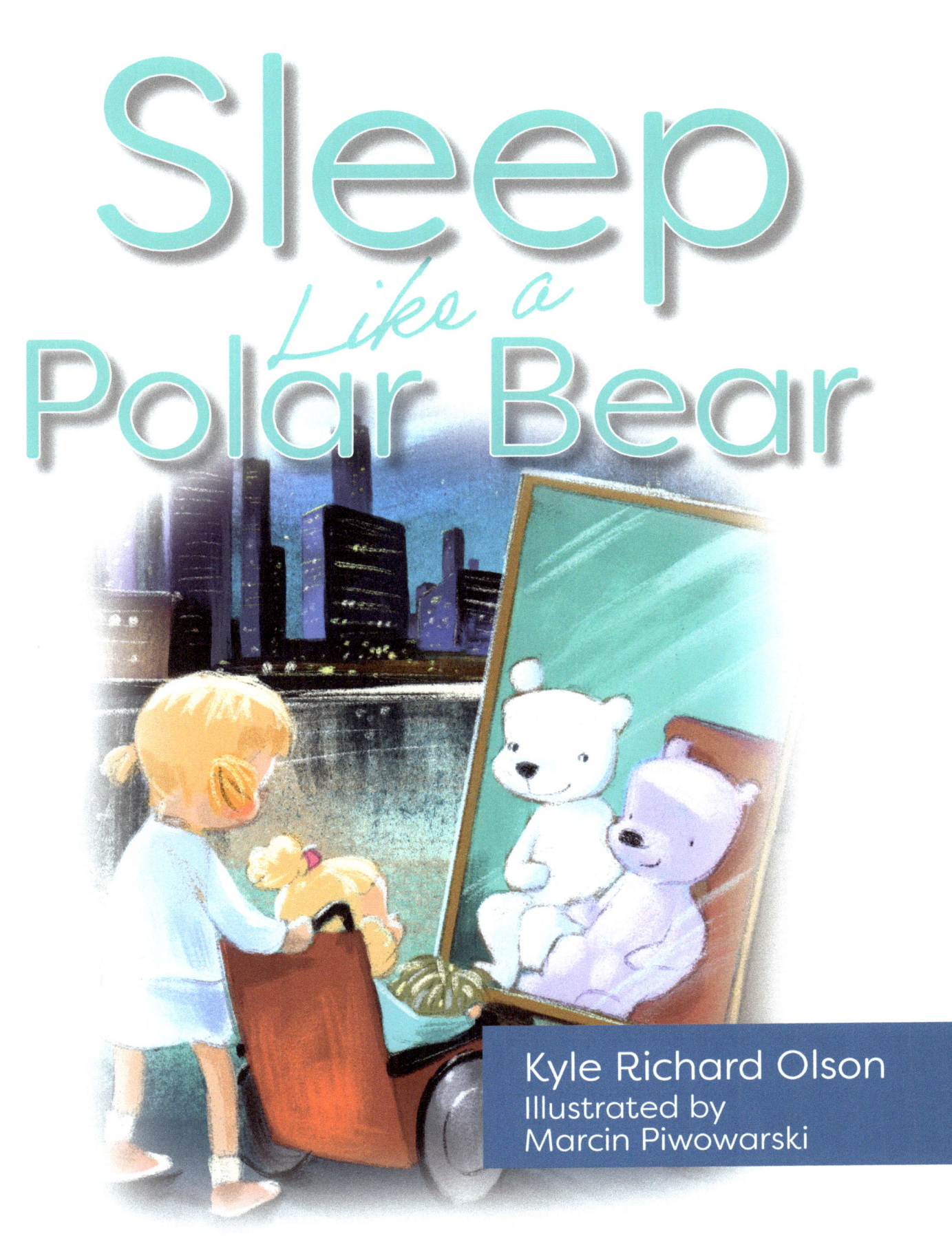

Copyright © 2025 by Kyle Richard Olson. All rights reserved. This book may not be reproduced or stored in whole or in part by any means without the written permission of the author except for brief quotations for the purpose of review.

ISBN: 978-1-963569-97-1 Hard cover
978-1-963569-98-8 Soft cover

Editing: Amy Ashby

Published by Warren Publishing
Charlotte, NC
www.warrenpublishing.net
Printed in the United States

*This is dedicated to the memory of my grandma, Joy Sandlund.
She lived out her name and left a loving legacy of the pen and the
brush, which inspired me to write a children's book. This is also dedicated to
all the true "polar bears" and their families, including mine,
who bravely, and often stoically, navigate the wild world of special needs.
Thanks to each member of that club for your poignant reminders that kindness,
empathy, and even humor can live, if not thrive, in life's hardest moments.*

There lives a little girl with the curliest of hair,
locks nearly as white as a polar bear.

Her name is Hanna, though her dad calls her "Pook."
She smiles and snickers because she just lost a tooth.

Hanna is happy and likes all her things—

her pom-pom,

her blankie,

her teddy that sings.

See, Hanna is sweet and asks not for much—
a song on the piano or a warm hand to touch.

But sometimes little Hanna, despite being so strong,
gets sick and goes away to fall asleep for so long.
This time, Hanna's left even longer than before
to the tall building with elevators and bright, colorful doors.

With Hanna went her wheelchair, her supplies, and her charts, but she also took her teddy for when it got dark.
Her mom and her dad, through all the procedures, talked a lot, even too much, about medicines and fevers.

They got phone calls from nurses, and doctors too,
all helping Hanna to make sure she'd get through.

And get through she would because she has a twin sister who is larger than life and very much missed her.

Her sister, Joanna, knows Hanna the best.
She knew Hanna was much tougher than the rest.

"Hanna is hibernating," Joanna declared.
"My dear sister's asleep like a polar bear."

"How right you are," their parents said,
smiling together and nodding their heads.

Then passed many nights, which felt like forever.
How long it had been since the sisters were together.

Joanna felt many feelings with each passing day.

Sometimes sad,

confused,

angry,

or afraid.

"You're not alone," said her parents. "We have those feelings too. It's okay to feel them. It's okay to be you."

"Because *you* are who we love, and your sister as well.
You're always safe with us and any truth you tell."

Joanna just smiled and sprang up to her room
full of excitement about what she'd next do.
She picked up her markers and the biggest pink poster
and drew her best winged unicorn for Hanna to show her …

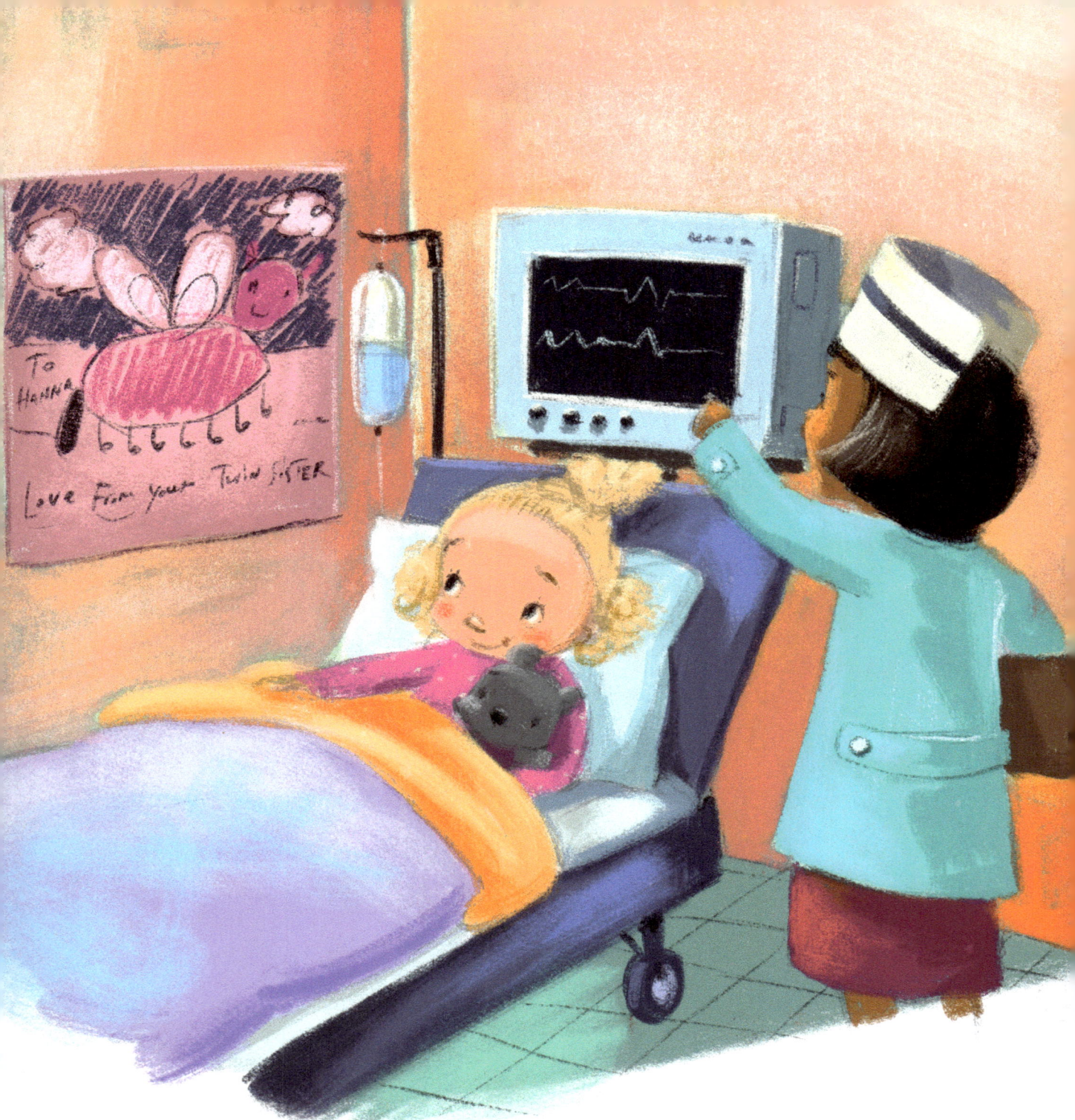

How much Hanna was loved by her sister at home,
to remind her through those days that she wasn't alone.
That poster made its way next to her hospital bed;
it gave Hanna a boost to lift up her head.

And lift it she did on one special day
when she smiled and snickered all of her pain away.
It was time for her family to pack the big van
and say "bye" to the hospital, with Hanna in hand.

She was ready for home, not a second to waste;
get the pom-pom, the blankie, the glitter and paste!
"Let's have a party for Pook and Joanna too!"
said her parents, more relieved than anyone knew.

So back home they all came in that van of theirs
with flowers, cards, and chocolates to spare.
All sent for Hanna, and her parents who missed her,
by people who cared, prayed, or lit candles for her.

All of Hanna's things went back to her bedroom—
plus equipment, bags, and supplies that were new.
The pink poster came too, that winged unicorn,
Joanna demanded it, then said something more:

"Hanna, this unicorn can fly high in the air in case you need it to fly away anywhere. Keep it for now, while I draw a new picture— of us, together, which best fits here."

So on a new poster Joanna then drew
not a unicorn, but a bear; in fact, she drew two.
As Hanna looked at the drawing, Joanna said, "We're there!
Both brave, done with sleeping—two polar bears."

www.ingramcontent.com/pod-product-compliance
Lightning Source LLC
LaVergne TN
LVHW060819240125
801963LV00011B/84